Tell Me, Tell Me

ALSO BY MARIANNE MOORE

A Marianne Moore Reader

O to Be a Dragon

Like a Bulwark

Predilections

Collected Poems (1951)

TRANSLATED BY MARIANNE MOORE

The Fables of La Fontaine

Tell Me, Tell Me

Granite, Steel, and Other Topics

Marianne Moore

THE VIKING PRESS · NEW YORK

First published in 1966 by The Viking Press, Inc.
625 Madison Avenue, New York, N.Y. 10022

Published simultaneously in Canada by
The Macmillan Company of Canada Limited

Library of Congress catalog card number: 66–23820
Set in Bembo and Fairfield Medium types by Westcott & Thomson, Inc.
Printed in U.S.A.   MBG

Second printing February 1967

Of the eighteen poems in this volume, thirteen first appeared in *The New Yorker*. The Notes and Acknowledgments at page 51 give complete bibliographical information on each of the selections in *Tell Me, Tell Me*.

Contents

TELL ME, TELL ME

Granite and Steel

Enfranchising cable, silvered by the sea,
    of woven wire, grayed by the mist,
    and Liberty dominate the Bay—
    her feet as one on shattered chains,
    once whole links wrought by Tyranny.

    Caged Circe of steel and stone,
    her parent German ingenuity.
    "O catenary curve" from tower to pier,
    implacable enemy of the mind's deformity,
    of man's uncompunctious greed,
    his crass love of crass priority,
        just recently
    obstructing acquiescent feet
    about to step ashore when darkness fell
        without a cause,
    as if probity had not joined our cities
        in the sea.

    "O path amid the stars
    crossed by the seagull's wing!"
    "O radiance that doth inherit me!"
    —affirming inter-acting harmony!

    Untried expedient, untried; then tried;
    sublime elliptic two-fold egg—
    way out; way in; romantic passageway

first seen by the eye of the mind,
then by the eye. O steel! O stone!
Climactic ornament, double rainbow,
as if inverted by French perspicacity,
  John Roebling's monument,
  German tenacity's also;
  composite span—an actuality.

A Burning Desire to Be Explicit

Always, in whatever I wrote—prose or verse—I have had a burning desire to be explicit; beset always, however carefully I had written, by the charge of obscurity. Having entered Bryn Mawr with intensive zeal to write, I examined, for comment, the margin of a paper with which I had taken a great deal of trouble and found, "I presume you had an idea if one could find out what it is."

Again—recently! In a reading of my verse for a women's club, I included these lines from "Tell me, tell me":

> I vow, rescued tailor
>> of Gloucester, I am going
>
>> to flee: by engineering strategy—
>> the viper's traffic-knot—flee
> to metaphysical newmown hay,
> honeysuckle or woods fragrance. . . .

After the program, a strikingly well-dressed member of the audience, with equally positive manner, inquired, *"What is metaphysical newmown hay?"*

I said, "Oh, something like a sudden whiff of fragrance in contrast with the doggedly continuous opposition to spontaneous conversation that had gone before."

"Then why don't you *say* so?" the impressive lady rejoined.

Although prepared for an "element of the riddle" in any poem, an even somewhat experienced person is not irked by clues to meaning. Attempting to provide a foreword to the catalogue of an exhibition of paintings by William Kienbusch at the Kraushaar Galleries in 1964, I referred to *Sound of the Gong—Buoy No.* 2. Mr. Kienbusch, himself present, remarked, "The partial arc—upper left of the buoy—suggests the buoy swayed by the sea and made to clang."

This expository aid made me profoundly grateful—like the following one concerning another composition entitled *A Small Island Fire:* "The smoke is a kind of shorthand for disaster."

I can scarcely be called *avant-garde,* and might say that "My Crow Pluto" is narrative, not an attempt at abstract writing. It says that crows entertain me, that the tame one perched on the shoulder of Barnaby Rudge lends Barnaby attraction for me; but that the bird has wings and should be finding his own food, not be encouraged to think he is a person.

My lines "Marriage," beginning:

> This institution,
>
> perhaps one should say enterprise

in no sense suggest a philosophy of marriage; are but a little anthology of terms and phrases that had entertained me, which I did not wish to lose and conjoined as best I might.

When John Freeman asked Lord Birkett (the British judge), "Why did you leave your father's business, to study law?" he said, "I think it was the fascination of using words in a way that would be effective"—true indication of indigenous talent. Ezra Pound indicates "passion" as at the root of the matter: no "addled mosses dank": "say nothing—nothing—that you couldn't in some circumstances, under stress of some emotion, actually say."

Writing is a fascinating business. "And what should it do?" William Faulkner asked. "It should help a man endure by lifting up his heart." (—Admitting that his might not always have done that.) *It should.*

In Lieu of the Lyre

One debarred from enrollment at Harvard,
may have seen towers and been shown the Yard—
animated by Madame de Boufflers's choice rhymes:
Sentir avec ardeur: with fire; yes, with passion;
rime-prose revived also by word-wizard Achilles—
Chinese Dr. Fang.

The *Harvard Advocate*'s formal-informal craftly rare
invitation to Harvard made grateful, Brooklyn's (or Mexico's)
ineditos—
one whose "French aspect" was invented by
Professor Levin,
a too outspoken outraged refugee from clichés particularly,
who was proffered redress
by the Lowell House Press—
Vermont Stinehour Press, rather. (No careless statements
to Kirkland House; least of all inexactness in quoting a fact.)

To the *Advocate, gratia sum*
unavoidably lame as I am, verbal pilgrim
like Thomas Bewick, drinking from his hat-brim,
drops spilled from a waterfall, denominated later by him
a crystalline Fons Bandusian miracle.

It occurs to the guest—if someone had confessed it in time—
that you might have preferred to the waterfall, pilgrim and
hat-brim,
a nutritive axiom such as

"a force at rest is at rest because balanced by some other
force,"
or "catenary and triangle together hold the span in place"
(of a bridge),

or a too often forgotten surely relevant thing, that Roebling
cable
was invented by John A. Roebling.

These reflections, Mr. Davis,
in lieu of the lyre.

The mind, intractable thing

even with its own ax to grind, sometimes
helps others. Why can't it help me?

O imagnifico,
wizard in words—poet, was it, as
Alfredo Panzini defined you?
Weren't you refracting just now
on my eye's half-closed triptych
the image, enhanced, of a glen—
"the foxgrape festoon as sere leaves fell"
on the sand-pale dark byroad, one leaf adrift
from the thin-twigged persimmon; again,

a bird—Arizona
caught-up-with, uncatchable cuckoo
after two hours' pursuit, zigzagging
road-runner, stenciled in black
stripes all over, the tail
windmilling up to defy me?
You understand terror, know how to deal
with pent-up emotion, a ballad, witchcraft.
I don't. O Zeus and O Destiny!

Unafraid of what's done,
undeterred by apparent defeat,
you, imagnifico, unafraid

of disparagers, death, dejection,
have out-wiled the Mermaid of Zennor,
    made wordcraft irresistible:
reef, wreck, lost lad, and "sea-foundered bell"—
as near a thing as we have to a king—
    craft with which I don't know how to deal.

Dream

(After coming on Jerome S. Shipman's comment concerning academic appointments for artists)

The committee—now a permanent body—
     formed to do but one thing,
discover positions for artists, was worried, then happy;
rejoiced to have magnetized Bach and his family
    "to Northwestern," besides five harpsichords
        without which he would not leave home.
For his methodic unmetronomic melodic diversity
contrapuntally appointedly persistently
      irresistibly Fate-like Bach—find me words.

Expected to create for university
      occasions, inventions with wing,
was no problem after master-classes (stiffer in Germany),

each week a cantata; chorales, fugues, concerti!
    Here, students craved a teacher and each student worked.
      Jubilation! Re-rejoicings! Felicity!
      Repeated fugue-like, all of it, to infinity.
    (Note too that over-worked Bach was not irked.)

Haydn, when he had heard of Bach's billowing sail,
begged Prince Esterházy to lend him to Yale.
Master-mode expert fugue-al forms since, prevail.

      Dazzling nonsense . . . I imagine it? Ah! nach
      enough. J. Sebastian—born at Eisenach:
      its coat-of-arms in my dream: BACH PLAYS BACH!

Old Amusement Park

Before it became LaGuardia Airport

Hurry, worry, unwary
visitor, never vary
   the pressure till nearly bat-blind.
      A predicament so dire could not
      occur in this rare spot—

where crowds flock to the tramcar,
rattling greenish caterpillar,
   as bowling-ball thunder
      quivers the air. The park's elephant
      slowly lies down aslant;

then pygmy replica rides
the mound the back provides.
   Jet black, a furry pony sits
      down like a dog, has an innocent air—
      no tricks—the best act there.

It's all like the never-ending
Ferris-wheel ascending
   picket-fenced pony-rides (ten cents).
      A businessman, the pony-paddock boy
      locks his equestrian toy—

flags flying, fares collected,
shooting gallery neglected—

half-official, half-sequestered,
   limber-slouched against a post,
   and tells a friend what matters least.

It's the old park in a nutshell,
like its tame-wild carrousel—
   the exhilarating peak
     when the triumph is reflective
     and confusion, retroactive.

An Expedient—Leonardo da Vinci's— and a Query

It was patience
protecting the soul as clothing the body
from cold, so that "great wrongs
were powerless to vex"—
and problems that seemed to perplex
him bore fruit, memory
making past present—
like "the grasp of the gourd,
sure and firm."

"None too dull to
be able to do one thing well. Unworthy
of praise, an orator
who knows only one word,
lacking variety." Height deterred
from his verdure, any
polecat or snake that
might have burdened his vine:
it kept them away.

With a passion,
he drew flowers, acorns, rocks—intensively,
like Giotto, made Nature
the test, imitation—
Rome's taint—did not taint what he'd done.
He saw as treachery

the all-in-one-mold.
Peerless, venerated
　　　by all, he succumbed

to dejection. Could not
　　the Leda with face matchless minutely—
　　　have lightened the blow?
　　　"Sad" . . . Could not Leonardo
　　have said, "I agree; proof refutes me.
If all is mobility,
　　　mathematics won't do":
instead of, "Tell me if anything
　　　at all has been done?"

W. S. Landor

There
is someone I can bear—
   "a master of indignation . . .
meant for a soldier
   converted to letters," who could

throw
a man through the window,
   yet, "tender toward plants," say, "Good God,
the violets!" (below).
   "Accomplished in every

style
and tint"—considering meanwhile
   infinity and eternity,
he could only say, "I'll
   talk about them when I understand them."

To a Giraffe

If it is unpermissible, in fact fatal
to be personal and undesirable

to be literal—detrimental as well
if the eye is not innocent—does it mean that

one can live only on top leaves that are small
reachable only by a beast that is tall?—

of which the giraffe is the best example—
the unconversational animal.

When plagued by the psychological
a creature can be unbearable

that could have been irresistible;
or to be exact, exceptional

since less conversational
than some emotionally-tied-in-knots animal.

　　After all
consolations of the metaphysical
can be profound. In Homer, existence

is flawed; transcendence, conditional;
"the journey from sin to redemption, perpetual."

Charity Overcoming Envy

(Late-fifteenth-century tapestry, Flemish or French, in the Burrell Collection, Glasgow Art Gallery and Museum)

Have you time for a story
(depicted in tapestry)?
Charity, riding an elephant,
on a "mosaic of flowers," faces Envy,
the flowers "bunched together, not rooted."
Envy, on a dog, is worn down by obsession,
his greed (since of things owned by others
he can only take *some*). Crouching uneasily
in the flowered filigree, among wide weeds
    indented by scallops that swirl,
little flattened-out sunflowers,
thin arched coral stems, and—ribbed horizontally—
slivers of green, Envy, on his dog,
    looks up at the elephant,
cowering away from her, his cheek scarcely scratched.
    He is saying, "O Charity, pity me, Deity!
    O pitiless Destiny,
    what will become of me,
maimed by Charity—*Caritas*—sword unsheathed
over me yet? Blood stains my cheek. I am hurt."
In chest armor over chain mail, a steel shirt
to the knee, he repeats, "I am hurt."
The elephant, at no time borne down by self-pity,

convinces the victim
that Destiny is not devising a plot.

The problem is mastered—insupportably
tiring when it was impending.

Deliverance accounts for what sounds like an axiom.

The Gordian knot need not be cut.

Profit Is a Dead Weight

Overinitiative has something to be said for it. With no resistance, a kite staggers and falls; whereas if it catches the right current of air it can rise, darting and soaring as it pulls and fights the wind. Overinitiative can take us somewhere. Humility is yet mightier, can sometimes retrieve a situation; as when the bear cub in Frank Buck's jungle camp escaped through a half-closed cage door, grew tired and hungry, hurried back, tripping over a python which looked like a fallen tree and reached camp safe, merely because the snake was asleep and moved but an inch or two. An exception doesn't prove the rule. The next python may not have just had a meal or may not be asleep.

I call these reflections "Profit Is a Dead Weight"—a sentence I happened on in my Italian dictionary: *lucro è peso morto*—because, although pride is usually regarded as the worst of the seven deadly sins, greed seems to me the vice of our century. Why should I pay "twenty dollars for the set" when I want *only* a portfolio, *no* paper knife and *no* brass gold pen? If I buy a chance and win a watch that was paid for by neighbors who bought a chance with hardearned money needed for food, did I profit? The root of the struggle to win something for nothing is covetousness. Do we have to be like the man who killed the hen who laid the golden eggs? Overcome by greed to want all of them at once, he found "only what he would have found in an ordinary hen. He had cut the magic chain and she would never lay again."

Behavior: it all reduces to a moral issue. We must not want something from another so much that we steal it; cannot kill another and benefit. Of morals bearing on sex, I hear more than I used to; of trial marriage as reasonable and different from delinquency, an evasion of the moral law, I would say: no innovation, and as old as mankind.

Among assets that one cannot ignore is the power of concentration. A preamble on television or snatch of phonograph music is not part of it. Are you able to ignore a disparaging comment, insult, slander? Smother desire for revenge? Make allowance for the defiant salesman who writes, goes on writing and will not look up? The traffic man hardened to explanation? The asset of assets was summed up by Confucius when asked, "Is there a single principle that you can practice through life to the end?" He said, "Sympathy. What you don't want, don't inflict on others."

In the last war, as a man who had survived a bayonet charge was thinking he might somehow escape, he heard a groan; then, "Nigger, pull this bayonet out of my chest." Hardened by the term of disdain, he hesitated, then pulled the bayonet out for the victim and "drug him a mile," as the story was told me. The surgeon treating the bayonet wound said, with a nod toward the Negro, "You owe your life to that man." The Negro and rescued man became friends and after discharge from the army, shared dinners and holidays whenever possible. "And do you believe that faked-up story?" I was asked, of a friend's factual report. How discuss verity with cynics—cynicism being a plant with no fruit or interesting seed? As Confucius says, "If there be a knife of resentment in the heart, the mind fails to attain precision." Defamation, denigration, ridicule, are easy compared with the ability to portray magnanimity—defined by a commentator (via Webster) as "loftiness of spirit enabling one to bear trouble calmly, disdain revenge and make sacrifices for worthy ends."

And what are worthy ends? Knowledge made possible by an overpowering desire to possess it; usefulness—like that of

Dr. Squibb, whose pure ether and reliable ether mask were "for use by all who needed them," never patented; conjoining bone and nerve ends of a boy's severed arm. Small (if small) ingenuities: one would like to have invented the zipper fastener, epoxy glue, the collapsible dustpan, figure-eight stitch closure of the hide cover of the baseball.

Sound technique is indispensable to the musician, painter, engineer, mechanic, athlete, fencer, boxer. One does not associate compassion, humility or modesty with boxing. Each could be "that talent which is death to hide" and a boy "wrapped up in it," speed-ball and pendulum, walking in heavy sand to strengthen the leg muscles; with an aptitude for "invention": a boy "coming up from a dungeon of darkness," in danger of being wasted, inhibited by false accusations—portrayed by Floyd Patterson in *Victory over Myself*. "It was a grind," he says, "but a way out for me and my family." The victory involved "application and concentration"—age-old formula for results in any kind of work, profession, art, recreation. "Powerful feeling and the talent to use it"!

"It should not be a case of sink or swim," Floyd Patterson says. "You have to learn to walk before you can run"; he (the pathos of it) having had to be *taught* to like being alive —at the Wiltwyck School in Esopus (New York), largely, he feels, by Miss Vivian Costen: "The only way I knew to thank her," he says, "was to be what she wanted me to be"; his repressiveness continuing a long, long time as "commensurate power" was emerging. Of coming to the Olympic Games he says, "I had to come four thousand miles to really begin to feel that I was like everybody else." Then, "When they handed out our official clothes, I could hardly believe my eyes. How do you describe the feelings somebody like myself can have at a time like that?" Having won the United States middleweight championship—never having bowed before—he says, "I placed one hand on my stomach and the other on my back . . . and bent low from the waist. . . . I don't know how long I remained in that pose. Long enough, anyhow, for somebody to say, 'All right now, Floyd.' Then I straightened up." The "feelings" are described "with perception at the height of passion"—letting Henry James say it for me. I doubt that anyone who is incurably interested in writing as I am, and always doing it, has had as much difficulty as I have in expressing what I fanatically find myself determined to say: How get it all in—compact, unmistakable —set down as if spontaneously? This book by Floyd Patterson with Milton Gross much intensifies my interest in writing—explicit, vivid, modest—every sentence enchaining the attention: "the dignity of equality" there on the page, for beginner or expert to examine at leisure.

After the conferring of contest awards for verse in a school which I visited, a teacher chiefly responsible for the zeal of the participants said in addressing the students: "You have daring, courage to believe in yourselves, craftly skill to produce that which is new and worthy of man as he was meant to be"; a combat warrant for scholastic effort applicable generally, one hopes.

"Recreation" can be punishment, and I have, like others, sometimes deplored television for misusing its possibilities. Sometimes, however, it has fired my imagination with gratitude as when I heard Andrés Segovia playing Boccherini, his fingers moving about among the strings of the guitar like hornet legs flickering here and there over a peach to determine its sweetness. I found absorbing also—although by no means similar—Mr. William Longendecker, an amateur of rhinoceros language, demonstrating his ability to mellow one of the animals by resting a hand on its head and imitating its speech.

Talent is a joyous thing—able to substitute the spirit of praise for the garment of heaviness; or so I thought when hearing—on television—Jean Renoir, son of the painter, interviewed at his home. Asked concerning childhood, "Would you say you were poor?" he said, "It depends on what you mean. My mother could do much with little. We were always surrounded by luxury in all that is done with the hand."

Talent, knowledge, humility, reverence, magnanimity involve the inconvenience of responsibility or they die. To the bonanza, the legacy, the professional hit, it would be well if our attitude were that of the Brazilian dazzled by unearthing a *calderão* (cluster of diamonds): "My Lord and Heavenly Father, if this wealth endangers my soul, let it vanish." It is what every poem is about, as Robert Frost writes, "the triumph of the spirit over the materialism by which we are being smothered."

Example is needed, not counsel; but let me submit here these four precepts:

Feed imagination food that invigorates.

Whatever it is, do it with all your might.

Never do to another what you would not wish done to yourself.

Say to yourself, "I will be responsible."

Put these principles to the test, and you will be inconvenienced by being overtrusted, overbefriended, overconsulted, half adopted, and have no leisure. Face that when you come to it.

Blue Bug

Upon seeing Dr. Raworth Williams' Blue Bug with seven other ponies, photographed by Thomas McAvoy: Sports Illustrated.

In this camera shot,
from that fine print in which you hide
(eight-pony portrait from the side),
    you seem to recognize
    a recognizing eye,
        limber Bug.
Only partly said, perhaps, it has been implied
that you seem to be the one to ride.

I don't know how you got your name
        and don't like to inquire.
            Nothing more punitive than the pest
        who says, "I'm trespassing," and
    does it just the same.
        I've guessed, I think.
            I like a face that seems a nest,

a "mere container for the eye"—
        triangle-cornered—and
            pitchfork-pronged ears stiffly parallel:
        bug brother to an Arthur
Mitchell dragonfly,
        speeding to left,
            speeding to right; reversible,

like "turns in an ancient Chinese
    melody, a thirteen
        twisted silk-string three-finger solo."
    There they are, Yellow River-
scroll accuracies
    of your version
        of something similar—polo.

        Restating it:
        pelo, I turn,
    on *polos*, a pivot.

    If a little elaborate,
Redon (Odilon) brought it to mind,
    his thought of the eye,
of revolving—combined somehow with pastime—
    pastime that is work,
muscular docility,
    also mentality,

as in the acrobat Li Siau Than,
        gibbon-like but limberer,
    defying gravity,
        nether side arched up,
        cup on head not upset—
China's very most ingenious man.

Arthur Mitchell

Slim dragonfly
too rapid for the eye
   to cage—
contagious gem of virtuosity—
make visible, mentality.
Your jewels of mobility

  reveal
    and veil
      a peacock-tail.

Baseball and Writing

(Suggested by post-game broadcasts)

Fanaticism? No. Writing is exciting
and baseball is like writing.
   You can never tell with either
     how it will go
     or what you will do;
   generating excitement—
   a fever in the victim—
   pitcher, catcher, fielder, batter.
         Victim in what category?
*Owl*man watching from the press box?
        To whom does it apply?
        Who is excited? Might it be I?

It's a pitcher's battle all the way—a duel—
a catcher's, as, with cruel
   puma paw, Elston Howard lumbers lightly
     back to plate. (His spring
     de-winged a bat swing.)
   They have that killer instinct;
   yet Elston—whose catching
   arm has hurt them all with the bat—
        when questioned, says, unenviously,
   "I'm very satisfied. We won."
         Shorn of the batting crown, says, "We";
         robbed by a technicality.

When three players on a side play three positions
and modify conditions,
    the massive run need not be everything.
      "Going, going . . ." Is
      it? Roger Maris
has it, running fast. You will
never see a finer catch. Well . . .
"Mickey, leaping like the devil"—why
          gild it, although deer sounds better—
snares what was speeding towards its treetop nest,
        one-handing the souvenir-to-be
        meant to be caught by you or me.

Assign Yogi Berra to Cape Canaveral;
he could handle any missile.
    He is no feather. "Strike! . . . Strike *two!*"
      Fouled back. A blur.
      It's gone. You would infer
    that the bat had eyes.
    He put the wood to that one.
Praised, Skowron says, "Thanks, Mel.
    I think I helped a *little* bit."
        All business, each, and modesty.
      Blanchard, Richardson, Kubek, Boyer.
      In that galaxy of nine, say which
      won the pennant? *Each.* It was he.

Those two magnificent saves from the knee—throws
by Boyer, finesses in twos—

like Whitey's three kinds of pitch and pre-
    diagnosis
  with pick-off psychosis.
Pitching is a large subject.
Your arm, too true at first, can learn to
catch the corners—even trouble
        Mickey Mantle. ("Grazed a Yankee!
My baby pitcher, Montejo!"
      With some pedagogy,
       you'll be tough, premature prodigy.)

They crowd him and curve him and aim for the knees.
                           Trying
indeed! The secret implying:
  "I can stand here, bat held steady."
    One may suit him;
    none has hit him.
  Imponderables smite him.
  Muscle kinks, infections, spike wounds
  require food, rest, respite from ruffians. (Drat it!
      Celebrity costs privacy!)
Cow's milk, "tiger's milk," soy milk, carrot juice,
      brewer's yeast (high-potency)—
      concentrates presage victory

sped by Luis Arroyo, Hector Lopez—
deadly in a pinch. And "Yes,
  it's work; I want you to bear down,
    but enjoy it

while you're doing it."
Mr. Houk and Mr. Sain,
if you have a rummage sale,
don't sell Roland Sheldon or Tom Tresh.
    Studded with stars in belt and crown,
the Stadium is an adastrium.
    O flashing Orion,
      your stars are muscled like the lion.

My Crow, Pluto—a Fantasy

Since runover lines in verse seldom read well, it suddenly occurred to me to continue a two-syllable-line, two-line stanza about a crow—My crow/ Pluto// the true/ Plato// adagio —but I am changing to prose as less restrictive than verse. I had always wanted a crow and received a mechanical one for Christmas. Then Pluto, whose rookery is in Fort Green Park about a block from me, adopted me—a dream come true. He may have been attracted to my favorite hat, a black satin-straw sailor with narrow moiré ribbon tied at the side, overlapping the nibs of crow feathers laid in a fan around the brim. If a feather blew away or partly detached itself, I had been dependent on a friend or relative to send me one in a letter. Now, I could salvage one almost any day from assiduous preenings—blue-green of the most ineffable luster. The hat—which had been bought me by my mother—was by Tappé, whose "creations" fascinated me, sketched and with descriptions by him published serially. Nor was the crow's intuition amiss, since he liked a great many kinds of food I like—honey, Anheuser-Busch high-potency yeast, dehydrated alfalfa, watercress, buckwheat cakes; fruit of all kinds.

Crows have a bad reputation as robbing songbirds' nests, fruit to be marketed, corn newly planted; even outdoing magpies in carrying off rings, gold thimbles, and gems, loose or set; but since this crow lived with me most of the time, I acquired what he acquired; inconvenienced of course by having to restore what I could, with somewhat fraudulent explanations lest the culprit suffer. Although Chaucer has the phrase, "pull a finch," meaning filch, official investigation of crows' crops reveals comparatively innocent ravages of farm products. Is not the crow, furthermore, famed as an emblem of Providence, since ravens—certainly corvine—fed Elijah; and "of inspired birds, ravens were accounted the most prophetical," Macaulay says in his *History of St. Kilda*.

My crow was fanatically interested in detail—the pink enameled heading on the stationery of *The Ladies' Home Journal* and the minuscule characters in *Harper's Bazaar* between the capital A's of *Bazaar* on that magazine's black-embossed pale blue stationery. I liked to take him with me on errands, although he attracted attention in a drugstore or store like Key Food, where I was allowed to bring him if I kept an eye on him. He, however, had an eye for too much—cheese, grapes, nectarines, "party rolls," Fritos, and gadgets for the house. He was, happily, as literary as he was gastronomic—very fond of Doctor Zulli's 6:30 "Sunrise Semester" on Channel 2: "Landmarks in the Evolution of the Novel," and would perch on a brass knob at the foot of my bed as I took down the lecture, greatly convenienced by having a companion who could supply a word if I missed one. Also, because it was near the typewriter which interested him, he favored a bust as a perch—a bronze by Gaston Lachaise (cast and given me by Lincoln Kirstein)—but I could not induce him to say, "Nevermore." If I inquired, "What was the refrain in Poe's 'Raven,' Pluto?" he invariably would croak, "Evermore." He understood me, and I him from the first, even if our crow-Esperanto was not perfect; two squawks meant "no" and three "yes," a system a little like reading Braille raised dots, or guessing the word left out of a familiar text in Poetry Pilot contests, indicated by the number of letters omitted. Pluto—or Plato—as was inevitable from his habits and proficiencies, became alternates; choice depending on the vowel in the preceding word; after "eraser" it would be Pluto; after "cubic" it would be Plato. Pluto, from the perch on my head, could see and pick up anything I dropped, eraser or pencil. If I said, "Dictionary," he would fly to my case of miniature books in the front hall and bring me Webster's *Dictionary for the Vest Pocket,* 3¼ by 2½ (1911), thumb-indexed and half an inch thick, containing "Rules for Spelling and Punctuation; of Parliamentary Law, of National Bankruptcy Law, Postal Rates, Etc."—heresy though it would be to mention Webster's Pocket rather than *New World Dictionary,* recently endorsed by me—if the Pocket really were Webster's "Latest & Best."

We should exemplify what we require of others and, having badgered a neighbor into returning a raccoon to the woods where he got it, I inquired one day, "Pluto, where were you born?" He said what sounded like "Correct account." I said, "Connecticut?" He cawed three times, so I took him to a Connecticut woods and liberated him—said, "Spread your wings. Fly," although "emancipated" is more accurate, since he was already free. "Fly?" Losing him was not simple but the spirit of adventure finally got the best of him. If what you have been reading savors of mythology, could I make it up? and if I could, would I impose on you? Remember, life is stranger than fiction.

To Victor Hugo of My Crow Pluto

"Even when the bird is walking we know that it has wings."
                                    —Victor Hugo

Of:

my crow
Pluto,

the true
Plato,

azzurro-
negro

green-blue
rainbow—

Victor Hugo,
it is true

we know
that the crow

"has wings," how-
ever pigeon-toe-

inturned on grass. We do.
    (adagio)

Vivo-
rosso

"corvo,"
although

con dizio-
nario

io parlo
Italiano—

this pseudo
Esperanto

which, savio
ucello

you speak too—
my vow and motto

(botto e totto)
io giuro

è questo
credo:

lucro
è peso morto.

And so
dear crow—

gioièllo
mio—

I have to
let you go;

a bel bosco
generoso,

tuttuto
vagabondo,

serafino
uvaceo.

Sunto,
oltremarino

verecondo
Plato, addio.

Impromptu equivalents for *esperanto madinusa* (made in U.S.A.)
for those who might not resent them.

azzurro-negro: blue-black
vivorosso: lively
con dizionario: with dictionary
savio ucello: knowing bird
botto e totto: vow and motto
io giuro: I swear
è questo credo: is this credo
lucro è peso morto: profit is a
    dead weight

gioièllo mio: my jewel
a bel bosco: to lovely woods
tuttuto vagabondo: complete
    gypsy
serafino uvaceo: grape-black
    seraph
sunto: in short
verecondo: modest

Rescue with Yul Brynner

(Appointed special consultant to the United Nations High Commissioner for Refugees, 1959–1960)

   "Recital? 'Concert' is the word,"
and stunning, by the Budapest Symphony—
   displaced but not deterred—
listened to by me,
      though with detachment then,
        like a grasshopper that did not
      know it missed the mower, a pygmy citizen;
        a case, I'd say, of too slow a grower.
There were thirty million; there are thirteen still—
healthy to begin with, kept waiting till they're ill.
History judges. It will
salute Winnipeg's incredible
conditions: "Ill; no sponsor; and no kind of skill."
   Odd—a reporter with guitar—a puzzle.
   Mysterious Yul did not come to dazzle.

   Magic bird with multiple tongue—
five tongues—equipped for a crazy twelve-month tramp
   (a plod), he flew among
the damned, found each camp
      where hope had slowly died
        (some had never seen a plane).
      Instead of feathering himself, he exemplified
        the rule that, self-applied, omits the gold.

He said, "You may feel strange; nothing matters less.
Nobody notices; you'll find some happiness.
No new 'big fear'; no distress."
Yul can sing—twin of an enchantress—
elephant-borne dancer in silver-spangled dress,
    swirled aloft by trunk, with star-tipped wand, Tamara,
    as true to the beat as *Symphonia Hungarica.*

    Head bent down over the guitar,
he barely seemed to hum; ended "all come home";
    did not smile; came by air;
did not have to come.
       The guitar's an event.
          Guests of honor can't dance; don't smile.
       "Have a home?" a boy asks. "Shall we live in a tent?"
       "In a house," Yul answers. His neat cloth hat
has nothing like the glitter reflected on the face
of milkweed-witch seed-brown dominating a palace
that was nothing like the place
where he is now. His deliberate pace
is a king's, however. "You'll have plenty of space."
    Yule—Yul log for the Christmas-fire tale-spinner—
    of fairy tales that can come true: Yul Brynner.

Carnegie Hall: Rescued

"It spreads," the campaign—carried on
by long-distance telephone,
    with "Saint Diogenes
        supreme commander."
At the fifty-ninth minute
        of the eleventh hour, a rescuer

makes room for Mr. Carnegie's
music hall, which by degrees
    became (becomes)
        our music stronghold
    (accented on the "né," as
        perhaps you don't have to be told).

Paderewski's "palladian
majesty" made it a fane;
    Tschaikovsky, of course,
        on the opening
    night, 1891;
        and Gilels, a master, playing.

With Andrew C. and Mr. R.,
"our spearhead, Mr. Star"—
    in music, Stern—
        has grown forensic,
    and by civic piety
        has saved our city panic;

rescuer of a music hall
menaced by the "cannibal
    of real estate"—bulldozing potentate,
      land-grabber, the human crab
    left cowering like a neonate.

As Venice "in defense of children"
has forbidden for the citizen,
    by "a tradition of
      noble behavior,
    dress too strangely shaped or scant,"
      posterity may impute error

to our demolishers of glory. Jean Cocteau's "Preface
to the Past" contains the phrase
    "When very young my dream
      was of pure glory."
    Must he say "was" of his "light
      dream," which confirms our glittering story?

They need their old brown home. Cellist,
violinist, pianist—
    used to unmusical
      impenetralia's
    massive masonry—have found
      reasons to return. Fantasias

of praise and rushings to the front
dog the performer. We hunt

you down, Saint Diogenes—
    are thanking you for glittering,
for rushing to the rescue
    as if you'd heard yourself performing.

Tell me, tell me

where might there be a refuge for me
from egocentricity
and its propensity to bisect,
mis-state, misunderstand
and obliterate continuity?
Why, oh why, one ventures to ask, set
flatness on some cindery pinnacle
as if on Lord Nelson's revolving diamond rosette?

It appeared: gem, burnished rarity
and peak of delicacy—
in contrast with grievance touched off on
any ground—the absorbing
geometry of a fantasy:
a James, Miss Potter, Chinese
"passion for the particular," of a
tired man who yet, at dusk,
cut a masterpiece of cerise—

for no tailor-and-cutter jury—
only a few mice to see,
who "breathed inconsistency and drank
contradiction," dazzled
not by the sun but by "shadowy
possibility." (I'm referring
to Henry James and Beatrix Potter's Tailor.)
I vow, rescued tailor
of Gloucester, I am going

to flee; by engineering strategy—
the viper's traffic-knot—flee
to metaphysical newmown hay,
honeysuckle, or woods fragrance.
Might one say or imply T.S.V.P.—
Taisez-vous? "Please" does not make sense
to a refugee from verbal ferocity; I am
perplexed. Even so, "deference";
yes, deference may be my defense.

A *précis?*
In this told-backward biography
of how the cat's mice when set free
by the tailor of Gloucester, finished
the Lord Mayor's cerise coat—
the tailor's tale ended captivity
in two senses. Besides having told
of a coat which made the tailor's fortune,
it rescued a reader
from being driven mad by a scold.

Saint Valentine,

permitted to assist you, let me see . . .
    If those remembered by you
are to think of you and not me,
    it seems to me that the memento
    or compliment you bestow
should have a name beginning with "V,"

such as Vera, El Greco's only
    daughter (though it has never been
proved that he had one), her starchy
    veil, inside chiffon; the stone in her
    ring, like her eyes; one hand on
her snow-leopard wrap, the fur widely

dotted with black. It could be a vignette—
    a replica, framed oval—
bordered by a vine or vinelet.
    Or give a mere flower, said to mean the
    love of truth or truth of
love—in other words, a violet.

Verse—unabashedly bold—is appropriate;
    and always it should be as neat
as the most careful writer's "8."
    Any valentine that is *written*
Is as the *vendange* to the vine.
    Might verse not best confuse itself with fate?

Subject, Predicate, Object

Of poetry, I once said, "I, too, dislike it"; and say it again of anything mannered, dictatorial, disparaging, or calculated to reduce to the ranks what offends one. I have been accused of substituting appreciation for criticism, and justly, since there is nothing I dislike more than the exposé or any kind of revenge. Like Ezra Pound, I prefer the straightforward order of words, "subject, predicate, object"; in reverse order only for emphasis, as when Pope says:

> Men must be taught as if you taught them not,
> And things unknown proposed as things forgot.

Dazzled, speechless—an alchemist without implements— one thinks of poetry as divine fire, a perquisite of the gods. When under the spell of admiration or gratitude, I have hazarded a line, it never occurred to me that anyone might think I imagined myself a poet. As said previously, if what I write is called poetry it is because there is no other category in which to put it.

Nor is writing exactly a pastime—although when I was reading H. T. Parker's music page in the *Boston Evening Transcript*, in what it is not speaking too strongly to call an ecstasy of admiration, to be writing in emulation, anything at all for a newspaper, was a pleasure: no more at that time than woman's suffrage party notes, composed and contributed at intervals to the *Carlisle Evening Sentinel*.

I am reminded somewhat of myself by Arnold Toynbee's recital of his spiritual debts—indebtedness to his mother for awakening in him an interest in history, "to Gibbon for showing what an historian can do"; to "people, institutions . . . pictures, languages, and books" as exciting his "curiosity." Curiosity; and books. I think books are chiefly responsible for my doggedly self-determined efforts to write;

books and verisimilitude; I like to describe things. I well understand the entrapped author of an autobiography in three volumes, who says he rewrote the first volume some twenty-six times "before I got it to sound the way I talk."

"Sweet speech does no harm—none at all," La Fontaine says of the song that saved the life of the swan mistaken by the cook for a goose. But what simple statement, in either prose or verse, really is simple? Wariness is essential where an inaccurate word could give an impression more exact than could be given by a verifiably accurate term. One is rewarded for knowing the way and compelling a resistful un-English-speaking taxi-driver to take it when he says upon arrival—dumfounded and gratified—"Ah, we did not suffer any lights."

It is for himself that the writer writes, charmed or exasperated to participate; eluded, arrested, enticed by felicities. The result? Consolation, rapture, to be achieving a likeness of the thing visualized. One may hang back or launch away. "With sails flapping, one gets nowhere. With everything sheeted down, one can go around the world"—an analogy said to have been applied by Woodrow Wilson to freedom.

Combine with charmed words certain rhythms, and the mind is helplessly haunted. In his poem, "The Small," Theodore Roethke says:

> A wind moves through the grass,
> Then all is as it was.

And from the following lines by Alberto da Lacerda (translated), one's imagination easily extends from the tiger to the sea, and beyond:

> The tiger that walks in her gestures
> Has the insolent grace of the ships.

Form is synonymous with content—must be—and Louis Dudek is perhaps right in saying, "The sound of the poem heard by the inner ear is the ideal sound"; surely right in saying, "The art of poetry is the art of singular form." Poetry readings have this value, they assist one to avoid blurred diction. It should not be possible for the listener to mistake "fate" for "faith"—in "like a bulwark against fate." The five-line stanzas in my *Collected Poems* warn one to write prose or short-line verse only, since my carried-over long lines make me look like the fanciest, most witless rebel against common sense. Overruns certainly belong at the right—not left—of the page.

Translations suit no one; even so, I still feel that translated verse should have the motion of the original. La Fontaine says of the adder that lunged at its rescuer:

> *L'insecte sautillant cherche à réunir,*
> *Mais il ne put y parvenir.*

In

> The pestilent thirds writhed together to rear,
> But of course could no longer adhere

the word "insect," so pleasing, is sacrificed; but "r," important as sound, ends the line.

Poetry is the Mogul's dream: to be intensively toiling at what is a pleasure; La Fontaine's indolence being, as the most innocent observer must realize, a mere metaphor. As for the hobgoblin obscurity, it need never entail compromise. It should mean that one may fail and start again, never mutilate an auspicious premise. The objective is architecture, not demolition; grudges flower less well than gratitudes. To shape, to shear, compress, and delineate; to "add a hue to the spectrum of another's mind" as Mark Van Doren has enhanced the poems of Thomas Hardy, should make it difficult for anyone to dislike poetry!

Sun

Hope and Fear accost him

      "No man may him hyde
      From Deth holow-eyed";
   For us, this inconvenient truth does not suffice.
  You are not male or female, but a plan
  deep-set within the heart of man.
Splendid with splendor hid you come, from your Arab abode,
a fiery topaz smothered in the hand of a great prince who
                                 rode

   before you, Sun—whom you outran,
   piercing his caravan.

      O Sun, you shall stay
      with us; holiday,
    consuming wrath, be wound in a device
  of Moorish gorgeousness, round glasses spun
  to flame as hemispheres of one
great hour-glass dwindling to a stem. Consume hostility;
employ your weapon in this meeting-place of surging enmity!
   Insurgent feet shall not outrun
   multiplied flames, O Sun.

NOTES AND ACKNOWLEDGMENTS

Notes and Acknowledgements

(A title becomes line 1 when part of the first sentence.)

Granite and Steel (page 3)
First published in *The New Yorker,* July 9, 1966.

See *Brooklyn Bridge: Fact and Symbol* by Alan Trachtenberg (New York: Oxford University Press, 1965).

Line 7: *Caged Circe.* See Meyer Berger's story (retold in *Brooklyn Bridge: Fact and Symbol*) of a young reporter who in the 1870s was unaccountably drawn to climb one of the cables to the top of the bridge's Manhattan tower, became spellbound, couldn't come down, and cried for help; none came till morning.

Line 9: *O catenary curve.* The curve formed by a rope or cable hanging freely between two fixed points of support. "Engineering problems of the greatest strength, greatest economy, greatest safety . . . are all solved by the same curve," John Roebling said. (Trachtenberg, p. 69.)

A Burning Desire to Be Explicit (page 5)
First published in *The Christian Science Monitor,* January 11, 1966.

In Lieu of the Lyre (page 7)
First published in *The Harvard Advocate,* Fall 1965.

Written in response to a request from Stuart Davis, president of the *Advocate,* for a poem.

Line 4: *Sentir avec ardeur.* By Madame Boufflers—Marie-Françoise-Catherine de Beauveau, Marquise de Boufflers (1711–1786). See note by Dr. Achilles Fang, annotating Lu Chi's "Wên Fu" (A.D. 261–303)—his "Rhymeprose on Literature" ("rhyme-prose" from "Reimprosa" of German medievalists): "As far as notes go, I am at one with a contemporary of Rousseau's: *'Il faut dire en deux mots/Ce qu'on veut dire';* . . . But I cannot claim *'J'ai réussi,'* especially because I broke Mme. de Boufflers's injunction (*'Il faut éviter l'emploi/Du moi, du moi'*)." *Harvard Journal of Asiatic Studies,* Volume 14, Number 3, December, 1951, page 529 (revised, *New Mexico Quarterly,* September, 1952).

Line 11: *Professor Levin.* Harry Levin, "A Note on Her French

Aspect," p. 40, *Festschrift for Marianne Moore's Seventy-Seventh Birthday*, edited by T. Tambimuttu. (New York: Tambimuttu and Mass, 1964.)

Line 14: *Lowell House Press*. Referring to a Lowell House *separatum: Occasionem Cognosce* (1963).

Line 17: *gratia sum*. Bewick tailpiece, "a trickle of water from a rock, underlined by heart in outline carved on the rock," p. 53, *Memoir of Thomas Bewick Written by Himself* (Centaur Classics).

Line 27: *a bridge. Brooklyn Bridge: Fact and Symbol*, by Alan Trachtenberg (1965).

The mind, intractable thing (page 9)
First published in *The New Yorker*, November 27, 1965.

Line 26: *The Mermaid of Zennor*. See "The Ballad of the Mermaid of Zennor," in *Affinities*, by Vernon Watkins (New York: New Directions, 1962).

Dream (page 11)
First published in *The New Yorker*, October 16, 1965.

Jerome S. Shipman's comment. In *Encounter*, July 1965.

Old Amusement Park (page 12)
First published in *The New Yorker*, August 29, 1965.

A Port Authority photograph given to me by Brendan Gill.

An Expedient—Leonardo da Vinci's—and a Query (page 14)
First published in *The New Yorker*, April 18, 1964; collected in *The Arctic Ox* by Marianne Moore (London: Faber & Faber, 1964).

See Sir Kenneth Clark: *Leonardo da Vinci: An Account of His Development as an Artist*. "Continuous energy. If everything was continuous in movement it could not be controlled by mathematics in which Leonardo had placed his faith."

Line 21: *Nature the test*. See Leonardo da Vinci's *Notebooks*, translated by Edward MacCurdy.

Lines 31–36: *"Sad"* . . . *"Tell me if anything at all has been done?"* To Dr. Henry W. Noss, Associate Professor of History, New York University.

W. S. Landor (page 16)
First published in *The New Yorker,* February 22, 1964.

See introductory note by Havelock Ellis to Landor's *Imaginary Conversations.*

To a Giraffe (page 17)
First published in *Poetry in Crystal* (New York: Steuben Glass Inc., 1963); collected in *The Arctic Ox* (London, 1964).

Ennis Rees summarizes the *Odyssey,* I feel, when he finds expressed in it the conditional nature of existence, the consolations of the metaphysical: the journey from sin to redemption.

Charity Overcoming Envy (page 18)
First published in *The New Yorker,* March 30, 1963.

Profit Is a Dead Weight (page 20)
First published in *Seventeen,* March 1963.

Page 23, line 19: *a teacher.* J. L. Fenner.

Page 24, lines 8–9: *"It depends on what you mean. . . ."* Interview with Winston Burdett, July 23, 1961.

Page 24, lines 17–19: *"My Lord and Heavenly Father . . ." The Diary of Helena Morley,* translated by Elizabeth Bishop. (New York, Farrar, Straus and Cudahy, 1957).

Blue Bug (page 25)
First published in *The New Yorker,* May 26, 1962; collected in *The Arctic Ox* (London, 1964).

Arthur Mitchell (page 27)
First published in a New York City Center souvenir program, January 1962; collected in *The Arctic Ox* (London, 1964).

Mr. Mitchell danced the role of Puck in Lincoln Kirstein's and George Balanchine's City Center production of *A Midsummer Night's Dream.*

Baseball and Writing (page 28)
First published in *The New Yorker,* December 9, 1961; collected in *The Arctic Ox* (London, 1964).

My Crow, Pluto—A Fantasy (page 32)
First published in *Harper's Bazaar,* October 1961, under the title "My Crow Pluto, the True Plato"; collected in *A Marianne Moore Reader* (New York: The Viking Press, 1961).

To Victor Hugo of My Crow Pluto (page 35)
First published in *Harper's Bazaar,* October 1961; collected in *A Marianne Moore Reader* (New York, 1961) and in *The Arctic Ox* (London, 1964).

Rescue with Yul Brynner (page 38)
First published in *The New Yorker,* May 20, 1961; collected in *A Marianne Moore Reader* (New York, 1961) and in *The Arctic Ox* (London, 1964).

See *Bring Forth the Children* by Yul Brynner (New York: McGraw-Hill, 1960).

Line 30: *Symphonia Hungarica.* By Zoltán Kodály.

Carnegie Hall: Rescued (page 40)
First published in *The New Yorker,* August 13, 1960, under the title "Glory"; collected in *A Marianne Moore Reader* (New York, 1961) and in *The Arctic Ox* (London, 1964).

Lines 3–4: *"Saint Diogenes . . ."* "Talk of the Town," *The New Yorker,* April 9, 1960.

Lines 13–14: *"palladian majesty."* Gilbert Millstein, *The New York Times Magazine,* May 22, 1960.

Tell me, tell me (page 43)
First published in *The New Yorker,* April 30, 1960; collected in *A Marianne Reader* (New York, 1961) and in *The Arctic Ox* (London, 1964).

Line 9: *Lord Nelson's revolving diamond rosette.* In the museum at Whitehall.

Lines 21–22: "The literal played in our education as small a part as it perhaps ever played in any and we wholesomely breathed inconsistency and ate and drank contradictions." Henry James, *Autobiography (A Small Boy and Others, Notes of a Son and Brother, The Middle Years),* edited by F. W. Dupee (New York: Criterion, 1958).

Saint Valentine (page 45)
First published in *The New Yorker,* February 13, 1960.

Subject, Predicate, Object (page 46)
First published in *The Christian Science Monitor,* December 24, 1958.

Page 47, line 2: *the entrapped author.* Alexander King.

Sun (page 49)
First published in *The Mentor Book of Religious Verse,* edited by Horace Gregory and Marya Zaturenska (New York: New American Library, 1957); collected in *A Marianne Moore Reader* (New York, 1961) and in *The Arctic Ox* (London, 1964).